For Quinn MW
For Oscar JR

First published in 2015
by Walker Books Australia Pty Ltd
Locked Bag 22, Newtown
NSW 2042 Australia
www.walkerbooks.com.au

National Library of Australia Cataloguing-in-Publication entry:
Wild, Margaret, 1948– author.
Bogtrotter / Margaret Wild; illustrator, Judith Rossell.
ISBN: 978 1 921977 55 8 (hardback)
For children.
Subjects: Children's stories.
Other Authors/Contributors: Rossell, Judith, illustrator.
A823.3

The illustrations for this book were created with watercolour
Typeset in Mrs Eaves
Printed and bound in Malaysia

1 3 5 7 9 10 8 6 4 2

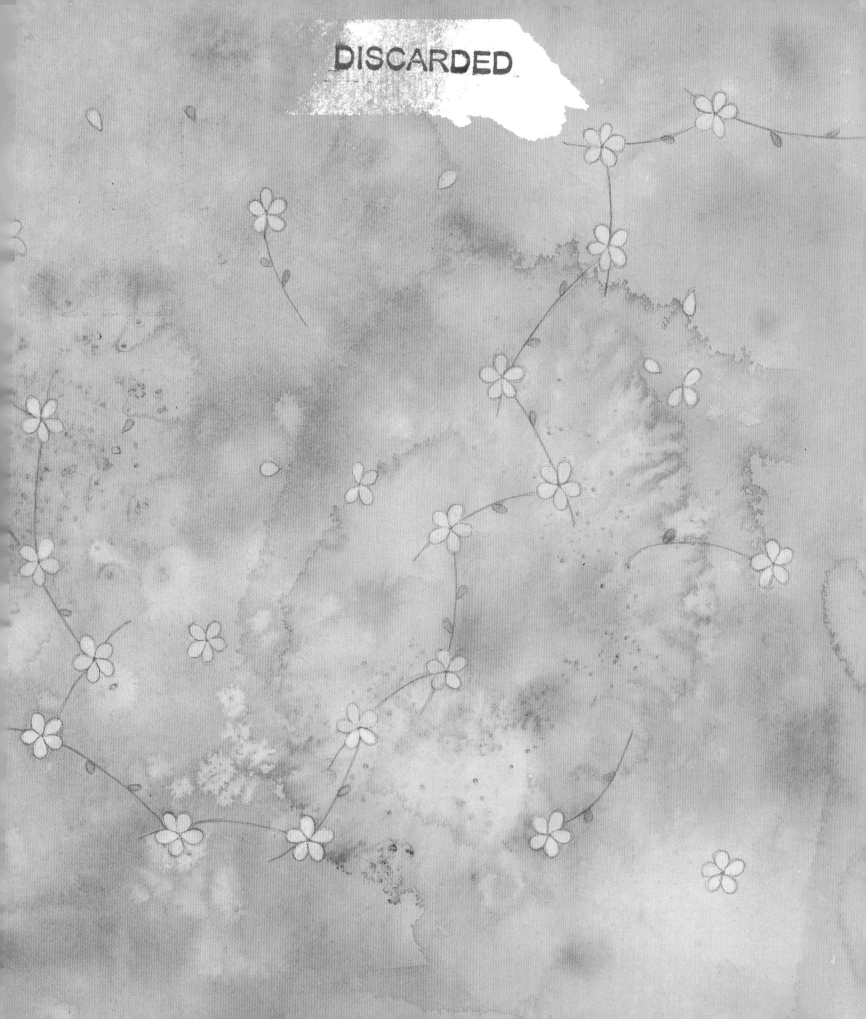

BOGTROTTER

Margaret Wild

Illustrated by Judith Rossell

WALKER BOOKS
AND SUBSIDIARIES
LONDON • BOSTON • SYDNEY • AUCKLAND

Bogtrotter lived in a gloomy
cave in a marshy, mushy bog.
Every morning he stretched,
yawning and blinking,
outside his cave.

Then
he started
running.

He ran across
the bog,
up the bog,

down
the
bog

and around
the bog until it
was time to go home.

He ran day after day,
week after week,
year after year.

Sometimes he felt bored,
but he didn't know why.

Sometimes he felt lonely,
but he didn't know why.

Sometimes he wished things would change,
but he didn't know how or what or why.

One afternoon, a frog said,
"Why do you run all day long?"

Bogtrotter stopped.

"Because that's what Bogtrotters do,"
he said.

"Don't you ever do anything new and different?"
asked the frog.

"No," said Bogtrotter.

"Ah," said the frog, and away it hopped.

Bogtrotter stared after the frog. He sighed. He shuffled his feet. Poking between his toes was a pretty yellow flower.

For the first time in his life, he picked a flower.

He smelled it.

He twirled it.

He stuck it behind
his ear.

"Ah," said Bogtrotter.

Then off he ran.

That night in his boggy bed,
Bogtrotter went to sleep
holding the flower,
his heart hopeful.

The next morning Bogtrotter
went running as usual.
But he made himself stop
to make friends with
a family of muskrats.

The morning after that
he stopped to swing
from a tree.

And the morning after that he stopped
to make a daisy chain of tiny pink flowers.
"Ah," said Bogtrotter.

From then on, Bogtrotter still kept on running.
Because that's what Bogtrotters do.
But every now and again,
he stopped to do something
new and different.

He stopped to splash about
with a family of ducks.

He stopped to dance
in the summer rain.

He stopped to slide down
a slippery bank.

And he hurried
back to fill his home
with bulrushes
and waterlilies.

He should have been happy,
but he wanted something more.
He just didn't know what or
who or why.

One morning, he saw the frog again.

"Do you ever run outside the bog?" the frog asked.

"No," said Bogtrotter.

"Why not?" asked the frog.

"I don't know," said Bogtrotter.

"Ah," said the frog, and away it hopped.

Bogtrotter stared after the frog. He sighed.

He stared at the flat green line of the bog
where it met the huge, blue sky.

Off he ran, as usual. But for the first time in his life,
he stopped at the uttermost edge of the bog.

Taking a deep breath,
he climbed over a rotten log.

He scrambled up
a grassy bank.

He clambered over
an old stone wall.

"Ah," said Bogtrotter.

And he started running.

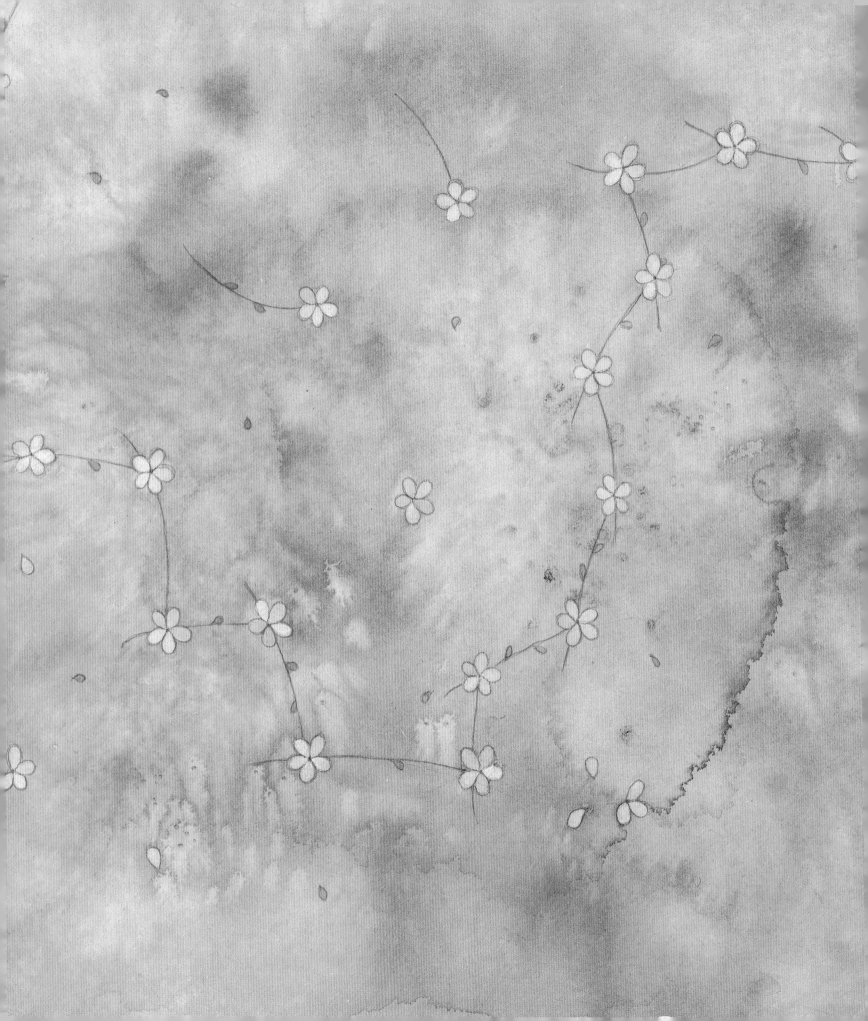